My Adventure

TIFFANY LONETTO

PUBLISHED BY

SIGMA'S BOOKSHELF

MINNETONKA, MN 55305
WWW.SIGMASBOOKSHELF.COM

My Adventure by Tiffany Lonetto

Copyright © 2020 by Sigma's Bookshelf.

Cover design contains public domain imagery from Pixabay.com.

Printed in the United States of America

First Printing 2020

ISBN 978-0-9987157-3-5

Prologue

Hey there, my name is Eva and welcome to my crazy adventure. By adventure I mean my life. It's not that exciting actually, being that I sit in my room day after day switching from Instagram to Facebook hoping for something new and exciting to pop up on my news feed. I have been locked in my house for seventeen years and many more to come I'm sure. A lot of things will weird you out, surprise you, or make you fall asleep during my story, and that my friend is why I call it an adventure.

Chapter 1

Welcome

My parents, Stacy, who is 46, and Bruce, who is 51, are total germaphobes. You are probably thinking 'Oh big deal.' Germs are gross, yeah, but this isn't what you think. "Germs" are the reason I have been locked in this house in New York for seventeen years. Our house is on total lockdown, and I'm not kidding. Our yard is sterilized twice a day. My parents both work from home, and if they're not on their computers they're cleaning, constantly.

My dad once got the flu in high school and he has cursed germs ever since. He met my mom around the time he was deep into research, and the stories he told to explain it all to my mom made her just as crazy as him. My dad was the stereotypical captain and quarterback of the football team. All the girls loved him. They were attracted to his good looks. He has light brown hair, pale skin, and almost neon green eyes. My dad met my mom, the cheer captain at the same school, at a football game. Guys would go crazy for her too. She has bright blonde hair full of curls.

All I have is dance and my sister, Ellie, who is my best friend; but what can I say? She is the only person I've got in this house besides my parents, and obviously I can't let my parents know half the stuff my sister does. Apparently we have other relatives, but we've never met them. Because of my dad, they probably think we're crazy too and just don't come around.

Me and Ellie once came across a storage bin filled with little kid toys and drawings. The pictures were of a little girl, who dad said is our cousin. She has passed now and he kept the stuff she made him. I wish I could've met her.

Me and Ellie think our parents are absolutely crazy for half the stuff they say every day, and we would both just love to sit outside for once and feel the grass between our toes. Yeah I'm seventeen and my sister is fifteen and neither of us have ANY idea what grass feels like, or even a leaf. Speaking of leaves, I once watched my parents scream in terror for ten minutes over a leaf that somehow got inside the house. Wild, but moving on.

This school year, my sister is going to be a freshman and I'm going to be a senior. We are both home schooled, obviously, which is nice; but it has its downfalls, like not being able to have any social interaction with anyone. I'm pretty sure if a boy who wasn't my dad ever walked up and talked to me, I'd probably faint. Even if me and my sister wanted to leave the house we would have to figure out the ten digit passcode to open the only door in the house. But then of course that leads to another door with another ten digit passcode. These two doors are on each side of a small decontamination room that sprays people down, then dries them off before they can come in our house. That's just how crazy my parents are.

People say me and Ellie look a lot alike, and they're right. The only thing that's different about the two of us is our hair length. Ellie has hair just shy of her shoulders, bright green eyes, and a perfectly straight smile. She likes dance as well, but she's more into the slower dances with the slower songs, and that's nothing like me. I love hip-hop, and listen to nothing but rap music. I am that basic girl who sits up in her room listening to music, imagining herself doing some life changing things to the songs, but obviously they never occur. My hair is light brown and full of curls. It rests about halfway down my back, but is almost always in a bun. I have worn baggy sweatshirts and shorts almost every day of my life, for as long as I can remember anyway. Ellie is all about fashion and trying to be exactly like the girls she follows on Instagram; but me on the other hand, I don't really care what people have to say about me, and besides, who is ever going to see me if I am not allowed to leave my house in the first place?

Our house has seven rooms and two bathrooms. There are four normal bedrooms: mine, my sister's, and my parents' of course. Then there is a fourth bedroom, which is made to look exactly like it does outside. Strange huh? It has fake grass, trees, leaves, rocks and even a river with running water. The water is sterilized of course! The next room is a room full of sterilized dirt, which is where all our food is grown. Then there is the med room, which has a nurse on hand at all times. This room is where we go if we get sick. If someone in the family falls ill, we stay in this room isolated away from the rest of the family until we know for sure we aren't sick anymore. My dad invented that room of course. And last is the cleaning room. It is full from the bottom shelf to the top-shelf with every different kind of cleaning supply any family could own. A room full of just cleaning supplies to get the house insanely clean.

Me and Ellie have been trying to get our parents to let us out of the house since we understood what was happening with our parents, and we have yet to be outside. I constantly watch out my windows in my room. What are the odds I have a room full of huge windows, but can never go beyond them? I find the littlest joy in everything I see out the window, from watching a couple walk their dog to the kids playing football on the corner. What I wouldn't do to play catch, or own a dog. Those are thing I might never know.

Chapter 2

New Adventure

Sitting in my room staring at the ceiling, I heard laughter. At first I tried to ignore it, but after a while my curiosity got the best of me. I went to the window, and when I opened my curtains saw a group of about five boys break dancing and hip hop dancing on the street. I had never seen anything like it before in my life. I was so interested in the dance, I couldn't take my eyes off the dancers. That is until I saw one boy hit the other's shoulder and point up at me. The two boys just smiled and waved at me like I was no stranger. I waved back and gave a little smile and by then the boy who was spinning on his head was waving along with his friends. They then signaled me to come down. I shook my head no, but they kept signaling. When I shook my head no again, the boys then waved their hands as if they had given up and skated off.

I closed my curtain and continued staring at the ceiling and began to wonder—what would happen if I ever left? How could my parents ever find out if they were asleep? Do they have alarms on my windows? What if they don't? My mind then began running through escape plans, and the pros and cons of leaving this house. Oh what I wouldn't give to have my freedom for a night.

The next day went the same as always, except it was my sister's birthday. To celebrate, the family gathered and played every possible board game in the house. We laughed and talked until neither one of us could stay up much longer. After all, that was a pretty busy day for me and Ellie. Usually we don't do anything besides sit on our phones during the summer.

Sitting on the floor drawing, I drew a beautiful girl dancing on the street with no worries in the world. That girl happened to look just like me. I then heard a noise. It was a rock hitting my window. It happened over and over again. After the third time, I couldn't ignore it anymore so I got up to go check it out. When I pulled the curtain aside and looked outside, I saw the neighborhood boys all spinning on their heads. When they noticed me, they stopped spinning, stood up and waved, just like they had done last night.

They signaled for me to come down again. As I shook my head no again, one boy fell to his knees holding his neck. He then fell over and all the others surrounded him. They looked so nervous and didn't know how to react and neither did I. I opened my window, and stopped to see if I could hear an alarm. When I didn't, I crawled out onto the roof below, then grabbed ahold of a branch of the tree hanging over the roof and slowly climbed down. I ran to the boy and pushed all the others out of the way. When I leaned down, I saw the boy completely content on the ground laughing. I was so confused.

This boy was clearly the biggest prankster of them all. He had short, black hair and a bright, white smile. He had tan skin, not super tan, but just perfect. He jumped to his feet and put his right hand out.

"Hey there, I'm Blake, and you are?" he asked.

"Eve," I said.

"Hmm, I used to have a dog named Eve. She died though," said Blake.

"Oh, sorry to hear that. Well, I'm going to head back in," I said, pointing to the house.

"Wait," said all the boys in a synchronized rhythm.

"I'm Adam," said one boy.

"Austin," said another.

"Mike," said the blonde one.

"I am Spencer," said the last as he threw me a wink.

"And we are 'The Boys,'" they all said at once.

"Nice, so you guys dance?" I asked.

"No, we just like to spin on our heads in front of a beautiful girl's window for fun. Of course we dance!" exclaimed Blake.

I just laughed along with the others. As I saw a light turn on in the house, my heart dropped to my feet. I then looked at the boys and ran to the tree I had crawled down. I began crawling back up as Blake rushed to me to try to pull me back down.

"I have to go!" I yelled.

"No you don't! I want to get to know you!" yelled Blake.

"I can't. I'm not even supposed to be out here—please!" I yelled helplessly.

"Fine!" yelled Blake as he let go of my sweatpants. I crawled up the tree onto the porch and stumbled into my room. When I got inside, I slammed the window, and shut the curtains behind me. I then laid down on the floor and pulled the covers off my bed and over me. My fast heartbeat started to return to normal. That is until my door opened.

"Eve!" whispered Ellie.

"What?" I whispered back.

"There are a bunch of randoms outside and they won't leave," she said to me.

"What? Where?" I asked.

She brought me to my window and pointed down at the

road I had just been standing on. The boys then laughed and waved at me. Ellie looked at me with so much confusion.

"Uhmm do you know them? Do you Facebook message or what is going on?" she asked anxiously.

"What? No, what makes you think that?"

"People just don't wave at any random person in their window like that!" she yelled.

"Shhhhh!" I said covering her mouth. I then shoved her to the ground and shut my curtain and sat next to her. "You will not tell anyone and you will not freak out, or I will even worse," I said angrily.

"Okay! Okay! What?" she asked.

"I might have just left the house to meet them on the road," I said, biting my lip and closing my eyes waiting for her to freak.

"Oh my gosh! Oh my gosh! This, this is great! We don't have alarms on our windows. I've been wanting to know!" she said, obviously enthused. I opened my eyes slowly, realizing she was more happy than me.

"You better not take all of them for yourself. I better get one and he better be the cutest!" she said, laughing. I just chuckled as she walked out of the room, giving me a big thumbs up before closing my bedroom door.

Chapter 3

Let it begin

I woke up the next morning and headed down to the kitchen to eat some vegetables and organic waffles, like I do every morning. You're probably wondering how we got waffle mix in the first place. Well, we have a maid who explores the outside world, then brings food and other things we need into the house. They then go through two full days of a cleaning and sterilizing process before they can come inside the house.

I finished eating and was heading up to my room when something fell out of my pocket and hit the floor. It was a crumpled up piece of paper. My mom shrieked then sternly said, "What is that?"

I slowly picked up the piece of paper and said, "Oh that? It was my gum wrapper from last night." I got up and walked over to the cabinet with the garbage can in it, opened the door, and calmly pretended to throw the piece of paper away.

"I'm going upstairs to draw. See you later," I said, then headed back up the stairs. When my room was in sight I sprinted the final stretch and slammed the door behind me. I then flopped on the bed and uncrumpled the paper. Written on it was a website name. I ran right to my computer and called up the site. On the front page was a picture of all the boys I had met last night. There were videos you could click on, and upcoming shows they'd be performing in listed, and even better they're all at night! The next one takes place tonight.

"Can I pull it off?" I said out loud to myself.

As I sat and thought about the whole ordeal, I then said out loud with a smile on my face, "Yes, yes you can."

The day seemed to take forever, but when it was finally starting to get dark, I went back downstairs for dinner. As usual, mother and father had little to say as we sat around the table and ate the meal our maid had prepared for us. When I was done I broke the silence.

"Mother, Father, I'm kind of tired this evening. May I be excused? I think I'm going to turn in early."

"Fine," said my father without even looking at me. My mother and sister looked up briefly as I left the room, but they didn't say anything.

I made my way upstairs and quietly closed the door, then spent what felt like the next hour in my closet trying on outfit after outfit until I found the perfect thing to wear. The show started at ten and I was so ready for it. I threw on my soft white dress and my light brown heels, then put on a few layers of makeup and threw some curls in my hair. I then grabbed all my pillows and made a body shape on my bed so if my parents did come in they'd think I was sleeping. I knew the last thing they would think of is that I had escaped.

I then unlocked my window and crawled out. I walked with my heels in my right hand and my phone in the other, then when I got to the tree stuffed both in my backpack. I then carefully climbed down. When I got to the ground, I tiptoed over to the sidewalk. As soon as I reached it, I dug into my bag for my shoes, put them on, and slowly walked down the block.

When I could no longer see the house, I dug out my phone and searched for the address of the show on Google maps. I then made my way towards the red dot on the map. It took longer for me to get there than it should have—about thirty minutes instead of fifteen—because I kept on stopping along the way. The trees, grass, and even the closed flowers were all so beautiful, and they were real!

When I finally arrived at the concert venue, I was extremely thirsty. So, I went straight to the concession stand and bought a bottle of water, then made my way to the back of the room and sat on a bench. This scene was much more lively than I could have ever imagined. The music was blaring. It was so loud, but surprisingly it didn't even hurt my ears. It sounded more like joy to me than music. I was so excited. The walls were all spray-painted. They had different words, shapes and pictures all around, some I didn't understand. People walked around talking, and some just stopped and randomly started dancing to the music playing. I could definitely get used to this.

It wasn't long before I spotted someone I recognized. It was Austin. He was standing with his back towards me talking to what looked like his parents. I started waving furiously and when he glanced over at me his face got beat red. He smiled and I assume told the people he was talking to he would be right back, then jogged to the bench and sat right next to me.

"Oh my gosh! Hello Eve! Does Blake know you're here?" he asked.

"No," I laughed. "No one does."

"I'm gonna go tell him. He's gonna be pumped! Talk to you later E," he said, then rushed off just as quickly as he had run over.

Seconds later, music started playing and the battles were just beginning. There were amazing dancers everywhere just jumping out of the crowd and taking people on. When it was 'the Boys' turn to take the stage, they were absolutely amazing! The tricks and moves they could do were unreal!

After they left the stage, I continued to watch. I couldn't take my eyes off the dancers. Until something made me. I got pushed on the stage, front and center, and I had no idea what to do. As I tried to leave, covering my face, people pushed me right back out until someone came on the stage to battle me. It was Blake. He waved his hands as if he was telling me to bring it on. So I did. I showed off every dance move I'd learned since the day I figured out how to do a search on the Internet. Me and Blake danced against each other until the very end of the night. Blake was voted winner, but I still felt like one. That was an experience I will never forget.

After the crowd had begun to thin out a bit, and the loud chatter had lowered an octave or two, I heard from behind me, "Now tell me where in the hell did you learn to dance like that?" As I turned around I saw Blake standing there smiling at me.

"The Internet," I said giggling.

"Well, damn! You better tell me what website you were on," said Blake chuckling.

"I can't tell my secrets or you'll be as good as me," I said, biting my lip.

"Ohhhh really?" he said questioningly as he got closer to me. "I would say even if I didn't win, watching you dance would still make me a winner."

Blake pulled my hips closer to his. I rested my hands on his chest as we stared into each other's eyes. Then the rest of the boys came running up to me and Blake, giving us each a huge bear hug. We then settled down on the benches and laughed and talked about the night and the competitors.

Looking down at my phone I realized what time it was,

two in the morning and I needed to get home. As I walked to the door, I saw the boys talking to some fans, so I just kept walking.

"Eve wait!" yelled Blake as he came running after me.

"For what?" I asked turning to see him.

"Why are you leaving? The party is just getting started," he said.

"I know but I never told my parents I was leaving. I just left," I said.

"At least let me walk you home. We live in a nice neighborhood, but not nice enough to let you walk alone," said Blake.

"Fine," I said as I could feel myself start to blush. He then ran to the boys to let them know he was taking me home. When he came back he grabbed my hand and led me outside.

"So tell me more about yourself," said Blake, as we started heading back towards my house.

"Well, I'm seventeen and dogs are my favorite animal. Speaking of dogs did you really have one named Eve that died?" I asked.

"No," said Blake as he laughed. "That's just something I say to a girl I'm interested in. It helps move the conversation along when you have something in common," he said.

"Well, Blake, if I were you I would search the Internet for new dance moves and pick-up lines," I said laughing.

"Ouch! That one hurt," said Blake, patting his chest. We walked and walked until we were back in my front yard.

"This better not be our last goodbye," said Blake.

"It will be if you don't find better pick-up lines," I said, winking at Blake.

"Well, just to make sure they get better, I'll send you some," he said, handing me his phone number on a piece of paper.

I just held the paper and smiled at him for a second, then turned and got a good grip on the tree and started to climb. When I was almost at the top Blake called, "Hey what's full your name?"

"Eve Marie Anderson," I said, "but call me Eva."

"Okay, well goodnight Eva Marie," said Blake as he did a quick dance move while standing on the sidewalk. I smiled, then continued climbing the branch. When I reached the roof, I very gingerly lowered myself from the tree and crawled over to the window, which I had left open a crack.

Crawling through the window I had the biggest grin on my face. I changed then hopped in bed to stare at the piece of paper. I ran my fingers over the numbers, then I picked up my phone to enter in the number. Then I sent Blake a text. It said, "Hey! I forgot to ask, What's your full name?"

"I was so hoping you'd text me Eva. I was afraid my pick-up line was so bad you wouldn't even text me to hear the others I had come up with," he texted back.

"Well, guess you're just lucky enough to get a text haha. Now answer my question," I texted back.

"Blake Jay Cooper," he replied.

"Well, Blake Jay Cooper, I never got the chance to reply to your wonderful goodnight to me. So, goodnight Blake Jay." I texted with my face lighting up like a Christmas tree.

"Goodnight," he replied.

As I read the text I smiled and shut my phone off, then set it down. I lay staring at the ceiling so beyond happy and full of joy I almost couldn't fall asleep, until I finally did.

Chapter 4

Better

I woke up the next morning and the first thing I did was check my phone and open up a text from Blake.

"Are you an omelet? Because you make me egg-cited!" Good morning Eva Marie. I hope you're eating omelets for breakfast, or otherwise I failed on the pick-up line again!" texted Blake.

I laughed and smiled as I shot him a text back. "No, Blake. I'm not eating omelets for breakfast, but the pick-up line made me wish I was!" I texted back.

I then set my phone down and headed downstairs. Ellie was on her phone and mom and dad were cleaning as usual. I then grabbed Ellie and brought her in the bathroom where I began to tell her everything. Ellie's face lit up just like mine had last night. We then ran up to my room and she helped me text Blake back.

"What are you doing on this glorious day?" Blake texted.

"Oh, you know, just sitting on my computer searching for some more dance moves," I replied.

"You can't do that, that's cheating! Unless you tell me which website you're on!" he texted.

"Sorry, no can do," I replied.

As the day went on Blake and I texted and flirted, and

I explained over and over what happened last night to Ellie. But really no matter what I talked about or to who, the only person I could think about was Blake and how he makes me happier than I have been my entire life.

It was about ten at night when out of the corner of my eye I saw a flash. It was my phone signaling that it has just received a text. It was from Blake. "Hey, since you haven't texted me in a few hours I was wondering if I could ask you more about yourself? Care if I ask a few more questions?" inquired Blake.

"I don't mind at all," I replied.

"Okay, hmm, I want to know your favorite food, dream vacation, and favorite color," texted Blake.

"Okay, here it goes. My favorite food is pizza, but I can never eat it. Dream vacation would be Bora Bora for sure, and favorite color is teal," I replied to Blake.

"How come you can't eat pizza? And I would love to explore Bora Bora with you Eva Marie!" said Blake.

"My dad is allergic," I texted Blake.

I was not about to tell him everything about my family, and that I can't even leave the house. Also, I would never invite him over with my parents knowing because he would have to go through the sanitizing room. It would be so embarrassing! Blake never replied to my text so I thought maybe he just fell asleep, but then all of a sudden my phone lit up again.

Blake's text read, "Look outside your window." I set my phone on my bed, put my hair up in a bun, and walked to the window. When I opened my curtains, there he was. Blake was sitting on the roof outside my window with a large pizza in his lap.

"Are you serious right now? You could get me caught!" I whispered to Blake as I opened the window.

"I paid eighteen dollars for this pizza, and I will either eat it to myself on your roof, Eva Marie, or you can let me in and share it with me. Your choice," Blake said to me with a grin on his face.

"Well get in here then," I said, as I took the pizza from his lap. It looked so good I couldn't pass it up. Besides, it is quieter in my room then sitting on the roof by my parents' window.

"Wow, your room is huge!" said Blake with enthusiasm.

"Thanks, and thanks for the pizza too!" I said with a grin, already digging in.

"Anytime," said Blake as he plopped onto the foot of my bed.

We just sat there, ate pizza, and talked. I learned everything about Blake that night and he learned everything about me, except about my parents of course. We then laid on my bed both ready to have a food baby from all the pizza we had just eaten. It was four in the morning and I wasn't even a bit tired, or was I?

When eight in the morning came along, I heard a knock on my door. I slowly stretched and started to get up, until I felt something. It was Blake! He had fallen asleep here last night and now my parents are at the door! My heart stopped. I pushed Blake right off my bed onto the floor, then covered him with my comforter.

"Shut up!" I whispered as I ran to the door.

"Who were you talking to?" asked my dad.

"Uhmm, no one. I was watching a cooking video on my computer," I said to my dad, stuttering my words.

"Why isn't your bed made yet? Do you seriously need help with making it at your age?" he asked, walking towards my comforter.

"No! I don't need help with it! I was sitting on it watching a video because my bed was too warm," I said running at my dad. "I'll make my bed when I'm done with my video." As I said that I could feel my face get beat red.

"Okay, we are having casserole for lunch and it will be ready at about Noon. Please come down then, and don't be late," my dad said, then exited the room.

I shut the door behind my dad and ran to the comforter.

"Get up! Get up!" I yelled at Blake, pulling on his arm.

"Okay! Okay!" yelled Blake.

"You need to get out of here, like now!" I yelled at Blake.

We both ran to the window. "I will go downstairs and distract my parents while you climb out the window and jump off the roof from the other side of the house," I suggested to Blake, pointing to the side of the house that was opposite of the kitchen.

"Okay, but I still don't know what the big deal is," said Blake, as he smoothed down his hair.

"My parents just don't like me hanging out with boys, especially in my room okay?" I said.

"Okay. Text me later?" asked Blake

"Yes, yes I will text you. Now get!" I said with a grin.

"Oh! And hey is your dad a boxer?" asked Blake.

"What? No," I said.

"Because damn you're a knockout," said Blake as he laughed.

"Get out," I said with an eye roll, as I ran to the door to head downstairs.

My dad probably wasn't expecting me for another hour, so when I walked into the kitchen, I tried to behave all nonchalant.

"Good morning Mom. Nice to see you again, Dad. I've thought of new feature we could put in the real room! Can you follow me?" I yelled at my parents.

They then followed me into the great room. I made up some totally insane lie on what I've apparently been wanting to add to the room for a while. It was good enough to keep them distracted for the ten minutes Blake needed to figure out how to get off the roof safely. I eventually felt a buzz in my pocket and looked down at my phone. Blake had sent me a text that said, "Gone."

"So what do you think? Can we add shelves to the walls to put my arts and crafts projects on display here?" I asked.

Mom and dad looked at each other and shrugged their shoulders. "I don't see why not," dad replied, "but the shelves will have to be made from wood harvested from trees in the backyard. I don't want any factory-made contaminants finding their way into my house."

"We can hire the same guy who cuts the grass to make the shelves," said mom.

I smiled and said, "That's a great idea, thanks!"

Chapter 5

Love

When I got to my room I went right to my bed to start making it. It wasn't long before I realized the pizza box from last night had been sitting on the floor the whole time. How my dad didn't notice that, I have no idea! Lucky I guess. I heard my phone buzz and it was a text from Blake.

"So your dad is allergic to pizza, and he doesn't like when you hang out with boys. He doesn't seem like a very fun guy I'm sad to say. LOL," texted Blake.

"Yeah I know, but I love him," I replied.

"I mean that's reasonable because every time you reject me and my pick-up lines I still love you through it all too," said Blake.

"Wait what?" I replied. "You love me? Did you mean to send that to someone else?"

"No, I don't have anyone to talk to besides you. No girl falls for my pick-up lines like you do, Eva Marie, and I'm totally fine with that," Blake texted.

"Well, Mr. Cooper, I will have to get back to you on that one. Haha," I texted Blake.

"Okay, okay," replied Blake.

"Do you care if I ask you a few questions?" I texted Blake.

"No, not at all. Shoot!" said Blake.

"Where do you live? What's your favorite animal? And if there was one thing you could change in the world what would it be?" I texted to Blake.

"I live in a mansion just down the block from you, Eva. My favorite animal is a lion because they're always fierce, and lastly if I could change anything in this world I would change your last name to mine, and make yours Mrs. Cooper."

I just read the text then dropped the phone on my bed. I had the biggest smile on my face I've had in a long time. How do I tell him I feel the same? I'll just have to I guess.

"Well, well, well, Mr. Cooper. I would love to visit your mansion. Doing anything tonight?" I asked.

"Only visiting my wife. How about you?" Blake texted.

"See you in ten!" I texted Blake, as I ran to my closet to get changed. I quick threw a big t-shirt dress on, put my hair up in a bun, and put some mascara on, then climbed out the window, onto the roof, and down the tree. When I got to the corner of the block, Blake was there waiting for me.

"I gotta say I am liking the dress tonight Mrs. Cooper," said Blake.

"Why thank you, Mr. Cooper," I said with a grin on my face.

"Now where are we off to tonight?"

"My mansion where I need to do some explaining," said Blake, as I noticed his face starting to get red. Seeing Blake get nervous and red-faced made me nervous. What explaining does he have to do? Does he have a girlfriend? Is he secretly part of a spy team investigating my parents? I asked myself these questions over and over in my head.

"Well, here it is!" said Blake

"Here what is?" I asked in a suspicious tone. All I could see were a bunch of businesses closed for the night and a box.

"This is my mansion," Blake said to me as it looked like he was on the verge of tears.

"The box?" I questioned Blake.

"Yes, sit down and I will explain," said Blake calmly. I sat next to him on the sidewalk as we leaned up against the building behind us.

"So, Eva Marie, I am not the person you think I am. I am a boy who sits on the corner with no food or shelter and begs other people for theirs," said Blake, looking embarrassed.

"Where are your parents?" I asked Blake, trying to put the puzzle in my mind together. "Did they kick you out of the house? Where are they? How long have you been living like this?!"

"Well, my dad is dead. He died in a car accident on Christmas Eve when I was three," said Blake, as his head started to tilt down. "Everyone else made it. Me, my brother and my mom, but not my dad, the one who deserved to live more than all of us. He was great," said Blake as I watched a tear fall from his cheek.

"My mom got bad into drugs after the accident. She left me and my brother behind at a foster home, and we haven't seen her since. Between the time I was four and when I turned eighteen, I lived in seven different foster homes. When I turned eighteen and they stopped getting money for me, they stopped caring for me too and kicked me to the curb. My brother is still in the home my mom originally put us into, which is too far away for me to visit him," said Blake, sniffling.

I felt horrible. I didn't know what to do, so I picked up his chin, grabbed his hand, and helped him up. We walked to my house where I invited him in for the night.

"You don't need to feel bad for me and invite me in you know," said Blake.

"I know," I said, as I crawled up the tree to my roof with

Blake following. It was going to be a good night.

* * *

"Okay, well since you are going to start staying here you need a bed. A private one in a place where my parents can't see you if they come in," I said as I opened my closet door.

"You want me to sleep in the closet?" questioned Blake, as he scratched his head.

"Yes. It will be warm and cozy, and a heck of a lot better than a cardboard box," I said. "Can you grab me those blankets there?" I asked, pointing up at a shelf I couldn't quite reach. Blake grabbed the blankets and handed them to me.

"Here," he said.

I carefully placed the blankets side by side on the ground to serve as a mattress. I then stood up and handed a bright blue blanket to Blake. "Okay, your mattress is ready, and here are your covers."

"Thanks," he said, wrapping the blanket around his shoulders, then twirling around as if he had on a cape.

"Are two pillows good Superman?"

"Yup, thanks. Way better accommodations than a box I can assure you," said Blake as he hopped onto the bed I had made for him.

"Goodnight," I said to Blake as I closed the closet door, leaving it open just a crack.

"Goodnight," said Blake, who was out like a light pretty much as soon as his head hit the pillow, or so I thought.

I turned off the light, then made my way over to the bed where my sweatpants and sweatshirt were laying. I sat down and had just started to slip my dress over my head when I heard the closet door creak open.

"Hey!" whispered Blake.

"What!" I whispered as I fell to the ground, frightened

that Blake had seen me half naked.

"I am not a photographer, but I can picture me and you together on that bed right now," said Blake with a smirk. Besides, your bed is much more comfy than the one in the closet I can assure you. Can I share yours until about three in the morning? Then I will hide in here, I promise!"

It didn't take me long to give in. "Okay, come on over and let's go to bed then," I whispered to Blake. I got up and climbed under the covers. Blake joined me and motioned for me to come closer and lie on his arm. I did and quickly settled in for the night.

It felt so nice to sleep next to him. I felt so safe and loved. I hope Blake feels the same.

When three o'clock came around, I heard the doorknob turning.

"What in the hell are you doing?" I yelled.

"I really have to pee," said Blake anxiously.

"Ugh! The bathroom is right outside the door to the right. Do not go beyond there or else!" I sneered at Blake.

"Okay! Okay! I won't," said Blake.

He left the room and headed to the bathroom. While I was waiting for him to return, I grabbed my phone and started scrolling through Instagram.

A few minutes later I heard something in the kitchen, and whispered to myself, "You have got to be kidding me." I made my way down the stairs and found Blake digging through the fridge.

"Get your ass upstairs right now or your ass will be back in that box so fast!" I threatened Blake.

"Okay," mumbled Blake, who had half a cracker sticking out of his mouth.

We got upstairs and Blake sat down on my bed. "These crackers taste stale. You really didn't have much for food," said Blake.

"I wasn't planning to feed you in the middle of the night," I said as I rolled my eyes.

"Oh my gosh. I am sorry. I am a nineteen-year-old still growing boy. What do you expect me to eat? Grass? I don't even think I could find one piece of that in this house either if I wanted to." Then the million dollar question came out of his mouth. "Why does your house look like it is on lockdown?" asked Blake.

"Because it is," I said to Blake as I rubbed my eyes.

"Wait what?" asked Blake.

"Since you were honest with me, it's my turn to be honest with you," I said to Blake, then proceeded to fill him in on my life story.

After explaining my situation, and telling Blake about my parents, he just sat there like he didn't know what to say to me.

"Now that you know are you mad?" I asked Blake.

"No, no not at all," said Blake. "I just kind of feel bad for you to be honest. It is just like me living in my box, only you can never leave yours."

"I know, it really sucks," I said as I tilted my head down.

"Well, if you could explore beyond your box, where would you go?" Blake asked me.

"Definitely a theme park," I said with a big smile on my face.

"You only live forty minutes away from one. Don't challenge me Mrs. Cooper," said Blake.

"I just know I would love rides, and the feeling of being free," I said to Blake with a twinkle in my eye. Blake looked into my eyes and smiled, then before I knew it he had swept me off my feet, and ran over to the window with me in his arms.

"Well, we can get married at a theme park in about a month or two. How would you like that?" asked Blake.

"What? A month or two? I don't even know you that well. Why would I want to marry you?" I asked.

"Oh I know you do because every time I call you Mrs. Cooper you freeze and smile with no worry in the world," said Blake as he leaned in close to me. I then leaned forward to meet him halfway for my first kiss ever with the boy of my dreams. I love Blake Jay Cooper and no box or parent can change that.

When I woke up the next morning Blake was still laying next to me on my bed. I smiled to myself, but only for a moment because then the door swung open.

"Why did the maid see your window cracked open this morning?" asked my father, who changed his tone of voice the second he saw Blake. "Wait who the hell is that?" he shouted. "Get the hell away from my daughter!" My father ripped Blake out of the bed.

Before I knew what was happening, my mother pulled me to the floor and dragged me to the corner of my room. I started to cry uncontrollably as my dad started beating, kicking, and yelling at Blake. All I could see was blood and all I could hear was Blake yelling my name, but it was fuzzy and distanced like it was part of a vision instead of reality. Once I snapped out of my daze and realized what was happening, I ripped myself away from my mom and ran at my father, who I shoved with all my might to get him away from Blake.

Blake was full of blood and could barely get up. I held my hand out towards my dad. "Stop please!" I shouted. At first my father ignored me instead of pushing me away. When I pushed back, however, he lifted his hand and hit me across the face as hard as he could.

I heard my mom shout, "Bruce!" as she ran to my side. I didn't want her to help though. I pushed my mom away as hard as I could and she fell backwards, crashing into a piece of furniture. My father ran over to her to make sure she was okay. While he was distracted, I reached underneath my bed and retrieved my money box with all my savings, then grabbed Blake and ran to the window. As I followed Blake out onto the roof, I turned back for a second and saw Ellie crying in the doorway. I waved goodbye to her and mouthed, "Sorry."

I knew my parents wouldn't follow because of the "germs" outside. We got down the tree as fast as we could and ran to the nearest train station. When we got there, Blake pulled out his wallet and handed it to me. He was in no condition to handle the transaction. He went back to holding his sweatshirt up to his nose to try and stop the bleeding. In addition to a bloody nose, he had a black eye, and scratches everywhere.

When we got onto the train, I helped Blake clean up. "I am so sorry!" I said crying.

"No need to apologize. It was your dad who hit me, not you Eva Marie. I'll heal quickly, but I think we should hold off on the wedding for another month. I want the wedding photos to be nice," said Blake with a grin.

"Ugh okay," I said with a smile.

My phone then lit up. It was my mom. "Where are you? Please come back. Your father will apologize. I promise!" she texted.

"No! I am done being locked up mom," I replied.

"We should go see your brother," I said to Blake.

"I will eventually. I'm just not ready yet," said Blake.

"Well then where are we going to go?" I asked Blake as I slid the power button on my phone off. It was the only way I could ignore the incoming texts and phone calls from my parents.

"I'm not sure yet, but I know we are not going back to that box," said Blake, as the train started to move away.

Chapter 6

Trust

"Wake up honey," I heard off in the distance as I slowly opened my eyes the next morning. Blake was staring right at me. "We are here," he said as I jumped up and looked out the window.

"Where even are we?" I asked Blake.

"Grand Central Station in New York, honey. We've been sitting at the station for a few minutes now, and need to get off before the train moves on to the next city."

"Oh, okay," I said, collecting my things. As I made my way towards the exit, I brushed by the very rude conductor who tapped her baton as if to say, "Hurry up, I don't have all day!"

Blake jumped down first, then grabbed my hand to help me down the stairs. After we jumped out, I just paused and looked around. I had never seen anything like it, and I had no idea how to react. "I know, amazing isn't it? Hungry?" asked Blake.

"Very!" I squealed at Blake as my stomach screamed.

We headed up the escalator to the street level. There was so much going on. So many different people, colors, styles, and taxis. I had never seen so many taxis in one place in all my life, not even on television. I just stood there not knowing where to go next until Blake grabbed my arm once again. "I know you don't know much about Central Station yet, but if you don't move with the traffic the traffic will move you in a not so nice way, so let's go," said Blake.

I don't think I said more than two words to Blake until we got to the coffee shop about three blocks away from the train station. I was just so amazed by everything happening in the big city. I had never seen so many people and vehicles in one place. Strangely, I found myself thinking about my parents when I noticed all the crumbs on the table. "They would freak out if they saw me here," I said under my breath.

"What?" asked Blake.

"Oh, I was just wondering what's good to eat here. I'm starving."

"Me too. Can't do wrong with bacon and eggs. That's what I'm going to order," said Blake.

"Sounds good to me too," I said.

As we waited for our food, out of the blue I asked, "So what now? I have never been outside, and now I am in a coffee shop in the craziest part of New York with a boy I fell in love with about a week ago."

"Well, I am not sure yet what we should do next, Eva Marie. All I know is I have just enough money for dinner and a hotel room for a night, then we need to hit the road again," said Blake.

"Hit the road again? Where do you expect to go Blake?" I asked, confused and angered. I was so overwhelmed by all that had just happened, and I was starting to regret getting on the train in the first place. I mean I am not eighteen yet. My parents could be sending out search parties for me. Or maybe my dad is beating my mom and Ellie because they can't get ahold of me. "I'll be right back. I have to pee," I said, jumping out of the booth and almost jogging to the restroom.

I checked my phone right away. I had twenty-three missed calls and almost forty text messages. They were from my mom and Ellie. I could tell they were both worried sick by the shaking voice in the voicemails from mom. I wanted to call her back, and I wanted to text Ellie to make sure they were okay. I felt as if the stall was closing in around me. I just slid down to the floor and let my emotions get the best of me.

"Ma'am are you okay?" I heard as I looked up to see this beautiful, blonde girl staring at me.

"Ye-yes," I said wiping my face. "I am fine." I jumped to my feet and sprinted to the bathroom door. As I left, I heard the door close behind me. I was faced with a major dilemma. Should I make a run for it and just go back home and try to make everything better, or keep running and make it all worse? I decided it was time to return home, so I headed towards the door leading outside. When I set foot on the sidewalk, I started running towards the street and when I got there I almost ran into the side of a moving taxi. The driver honked his horn, which stopped me in my tracks. As I turned around, I saw Blake looking at me from the doorway of the coffee shop. He jumped to his feet to chase after me, so I ran.

I kept running and eventually made a wrong turn, ending up at the dead end in a random alley. Blake, who was shortly behind me, caught up with me there and grabbed me. "Get the hell off of me!" I yelled as I shoved Blake off of me.

"Eva, calm down! What is going on? What the hell was that?" asked Blake angrily as he pointed to the open alley.

"I want to go home. I don't want to run anymore," I said, falling to my knees as my teardrops hit the blacktop below me.

Blake leaned against the brick wall next to me and calmly said, "Listen, I know you are scared and your mind is going crazy right now. Mine is too and I didn't even leave any family behind, but look at my face," said Blake, grabbing my face and forcing me to look directly at him.. "This is what yours will look like if you go back Eva. I mean I am not going to force you to run, but don't you think running is better than going back and living in the same old abusive box you have been in for seventeen years? Don't think I didn't realize the makeup on your face and your wrist was covering up bruises. Your dad abuses you and that is not okay!" said Blake, grabbing my hand. I was so embarrassed that he found out my darkest secret, let alone he knew the whole time. But he was right. If I go back it is only going to get worse.

"Can we go get food?" I asked with a giggle, holding my belly.

"Yes we can, Eva. Even though you just earned the waitress a thirty dollar tip for hopefully keeping our order," Blake said with a chuckle as we stood up and walked back to the coffee shop.

After we ate, we left the cafe and for the first time in a long time my belly was completely full. As it started to get dark fast, we walked to the nearest hotel and got a room for the night. Everything was so fancy there, and not just because it was the first hotel I had ever been in. It just seemed pretty high class. We got the keys to our room and headed up in the elevator. When we got to the room it felt odd. I had nothing but my backpack, and the only thing in that was my box of money. I opened a drawer near the bed and hid it inside, then went to check out the bathroom. "I think I am going to shower," I yelled to Blake, who was already lying on the bed.

"Sounds good, but come here first," said Blake. I came out and sat on the bed next to him. "Are you okay now?" asked Blake, who had a sweet smile on his face.

"Yes, yes I'm fine. I am sorry about earlier," I said embarrassed.

"No. Don't apologize. It is okay. I get it. The situation you're in is overwhelming," said Blake, looking at me.

I didn't know what to say back, so instead I focused on the task on hand. "Well, I am going to shower," I said to Blake as I hopped off the bed.

"Here," said Blake, handing me a big t-shirt.

"What's this for?" I questioned Blake.

"Your clothes are filthy. Your shirt has a huge ketchup stain from dinner," Blake said with a chuckle.

"You know what? That burger was amazing. Thank you very much!" I said with a grin as I snatched the shirt from him.

"They have a washer and dryer here. While you're in the shower I'll throw our clothes in so they are clean for tomorrow," said Blake. He was so caring. I mean what boy offers to do a girl's laundry?

"That sounds great," I said, walking around the bed. I grabbed a five dollar bill and tossed it at him. "Here, use this. You have to let me pay for something." I grinned at Blake as I headed towards the bathroom.

"Just throw your clothes outside the door before you hop in the shower. While you're washing up, I'll head downstairs to do the laundry," said Blake. I closed the door and looked into the mirror. All I could think about was what the hell was I doing? How did Blake get so tied in with all of this, and how in the world could I love and trust someone this much already?

A few minutes passed, and my trance was eventually broken when Blake called out, "If you prefer I can come in the bathroom and get them myself."

"No need. They'll be out in a minute," I said through the crack in the door. I shut it fully, then undressed and grabbed a towel to wrap around myself. I then picked up the clothes on the floor, cracked the door open a tiny bit, and tossed them towards the bed. "Here you go, thanks!"

I then closed the door and headed towards the shower. I turned it on and waited for the water to warm up to the perfect temperature. Once it did, I dropped the towel to the floor and stepped in. The shower felt amazing! I stood there for what felt like hours as the warm water massaged my tired muscles. When I finally got out the mirror was so fogged up I just laughed. As I put Blake's t-shirt on, I smiled when I realized it fit perfectly, just like a nightgown. I then brushed my hair before opening the door back into the bedroom.

Blake still wasn't back, so I jumped in bed and turned on the television. I was flipping through channels until something caught my eye on Channel 3, which was where FOX 21 News was on cable. When I switched back I saw something that made my stomach drop. It was my dad. He was standing outside our house being interviewed. The title, 'Missing girl, 17, Eva Anderson,' appeared at the bottom of the screen. My heart stopped and my stomach dropped as Blake walked in with our clothes in one hand and snacks from the vending machine in the other. He just stood with the door open and watched with me. We were both so in shock until my dad said, "Oh yeah. She will be in very big trouble when she gets home. The sooner the better for her though," he added as he grabbed a tissue and pretended to cry. I had chills all over my body. My cheeks were soaked from tears. Blake dropped everything in the doorway and ran to me, grabbing me and hugging me tight. I was waiting for him to say something, but he never did.

Chapter 7

Decisions

When I woke up the next morning my head was pounding. As if he had anticipated my needs, Blake was sitting at the foot of the bed holding a tray of breakfast food. "I got you a little bit of everything, and some ketchup packets because I saw the way you loaded that burger last night," said Blake with a chuckle.

"Thanks," I said, grabbing the tray.

As I started to eat my breakfast, Blake said, "What if we do go to Bora Bora, Eva? I mean really what if we do?"

"You can't be serious, Blake," I said, rolling my eyes. "This is no time to be sarcastic. I'm going home. I have to," I said in a stern voice.

"Wait! What? No! You are not going back—"

"And what happens if I don't Blake? You think they will all forget about me and let it go? No, my dad is probably using Ellie as his punching his bag now. So I'll just return home, and help take the edge off her," I said disappointedly.

"No! You are not going anywhere!" said Blake.

"What do you want out of this Blake? Me? Why? I am meant to be locked up in that house. That is who I was born to be and I need to go back. What makes you think you can just say you love me and everything will work out? No, Blake. It won't work. We're too young to make it on our own. We have to give up!" I yelled.

"Wow, Eva! I believe you are destined to do more than just sit in that house of yours. You were destined to make a difference in this world, and even if you don't see that it's okay because everyone else can! I have felt alone for so many years, and when I found you, you saved me. You helped me smile again. You made me feel loved and wanted when no one else would even acknowledge me, and if you can't see that then I just don't know." Tears rolled down Blake's cheeks as he spoke." Be sure that going back is the right choice because if you do, you may never get the chance to make a life for yourself again!"

Blake set something down on the table, sniffled, then picked up his bag and walked out the door. I got up and walked over to the table. He had left a round trip flight ticket to Bora Bora behind. It was at that moment that I made my decision. I grabbed my box of money, threw it in my backpack, and ran to the elevator. When I got to the lobby, I could not spot Blake anywhere. So, I ran outside. When I looked to the right, I saw him down the block climbing into a taxi. I ran towards him as fast as I could and shouted, "Blake!" as loud as I could. Fortunately, he heard me. He got back out of the taxi, shut the door, and waved it off. When our noses were almost touching I said, "I'll go with you on one condition."

"What's that?" asked Blake.

"We get Ellie first."

* * *

"So are you sure about this?" asked Blake, as we rode the escalator down to the train platform.

"Yes, one hundred percent," I said with a grin. We hopped onto the train, found an empty pair of seats and sat down. As the train started to pull out of the station I asked Blake, "So what is the plan?"

"I don't know," said Blake.

"Well, good thing we have a half hour to figure one out," I said with a grin. Me and Blake started brainstorming, and by the time the train pulled into the station where this whole adventure had begun we had a plan.

I sent Ellie a text saying, "I'm home."

Not even a minute later I got one back that said, "Oh my God, where? Do not come in the house. There are alarms and traps everywhere. Dad is preparing for you!"

I replied, "Pack a bag Ellie, and pack me a few of my things too please."

"I will never be able to get out. What if he catches me, or even worse you?" Ellie replied.

"It will be okay. Trust me and start packing now," I texted. I waited, but she didn't reply. When we got to the house, so much was different. All of the windows were tinted. The tree I used to climb down had been cut to the ground. The grass was dead, and we had a real door. I walked around to the other side of the house and climbed up the fence, then onto the roof from there. I went up to my bedroom window where I saw everything boxed up. My room was empty. I just looked in the window so confused, and aggravated until my phone lit up. I looked down. It was a text from Ellie that said, "RUN!"

Before I could react, the window shattered. I threw my hands up in front of my face and rolled back on the roof. My dad crawled out of the window with a hammer in his hand and came at me. Before I knew it, he was on top of me and about to clobber me in the face with the hammer, but Blake came out of nowhere and stopped him. I got up quickly, grabbed the hammer and proceeded to throw it off the roof to the ground. As Blake and my dad were wrestling on the roof, I ran over to see my mom and Ellie standing on the other side, screaming at my dad to stop. I grabbed the backpack from Ellie and pulled her out. I grabbed mom and hugged her as hard as I could and she did the same. She then grabbed my face and said, "Run as fast as you can and protect her!"

"I will mom, I will. I love you," I said, falling apart.

"I love you too honey. Goodbye," said mom. When I went to grab Ellie's arm she screamed in pain. She was completely covered in bruises. She had two black eyes and a brace around her wrist. My face then turned beat red. I felt my blood start to boil.

I looked over to see my dad on top of Blake, punching him. I was so angry I ran over and jumped into the fray. It was just the distraction Blake needed to slip away, and my dad and I went at it. We punched and kicked each other as hard as we could. I was hanging in there until he kicked me hard in the side. I rolled away and unable to get my bearings, I tumbled off the roof. When I came to a rest on the ground below, I heard nothing but screaming and high pitched tones. I saw nothing but grass and blur, then I blacked out.

When I woke up, there was a random woman standing over me. I had no idea who she was, so I tried to jump to my feet, but couldn't. She pushed me back down on the bed and held me there until someone came in the room. It was Blake. He ran to me and grabbed me. He was crying. "Are you okay? Do you remember me? I love you so much! Eva Marie talk to me!"

"Where am I?" I asked, confused.

"We're still in New York. Just the part no one knows about," said Blake.

"Where the hell is Ellie?" I replied, trying to jump up again, but unable to do so due to the pain in my side.

"She's okay! She's okay! You need to relax. She is sleeping in the other room. She's alright. We got her," said Blake, brushing my hair back.

"Where is my dad? Did he hurt her?" I asked.

"He's gone. He won't find us here, or at least where we are going to go next," said Blake.

"Where? Bora Bora?" I asked.

"No, we are going to Connecticut if that's okay with you," said Blake with a complete smile.

"Why Connecticut?" I asked.

"Dalton is there," said Blake smiling.

"W—who is Dalton? I replied.

"My brother," said Blake smiling. I just laid my head back and smiled. Maybe Blake was right. Maybe everything is going to work out in the end. At least I hope it will.

Chapter 8

Let's go

"Who was that lady?" I asked Blake as we walked down the sidewalk to the train station.

"She's the social worker who helped me grow up, fed me and cared for me when I really, really needed it," said Blake.

"What the hell happened after I fell off the roof?" I asked.

"You blacked out. Your whole body went numb and me and Ellie carried you while your mom distracted you dad," said Blake.

"Mom missed you so much," said Ellie, "but she always said to me she knew you'd come back for me. I'm so glad she was right. Dad was so terrifying. He never slept and he drank so much," said Ellie.

"What was he drinking? Was it sterilized" I asked with a giggle.

"I don't know what it was, but it didn't go well with his temper. He'd wake me up out of a dead sleep with a hard hit to the face or stomach," said Ellie with her head down, looking at her feet.

I began to cry and whimpered, "I am so sorry, Ellie! I never should have left you alone with him! It's my fault you—"

"Stop that!" said Blake sternly. "What happened to you

and Ellie and your mom is not your fault! Nobody deserves to be treated the way your father has treated you! I hope he rots in prison!"

"Wait! Is he in jail?" I asked, unaware of what had happened to him after the beating.

"Yes, exactly where he belongs," said Ellie.

"What about mom?"

"She's someplace safe. He won't be able to hurt her ever again," said Blake.

When we boarded the train, I plopped into my seat right next to Ellie. It took us each about fifteen minutes into the ride before passing out. When we woke up we were just twenty minutes from Connecticut. I looked across the aisle to see Blake staring out the window, looking like he was on the verge of tears. "What's going on?" I asked, jumping into the seat next to him.

"I'm so damn scared, Eva. I've been waiting for this moment since the day I left his side. I don't know if I'm ready. What if he didn't miss me? Or doesn't want to see me? What if he hates me?" asked Blake with a tear falling down his cheek.

"I've known you for about a month and you have shown me just about everything I need to know. You saved me from my father, who used me as a punching bag for his problems. You showed me how to stand up for myself and not back down. You're an amazing person, Blake, and anyone would be silly to not realize that, especially your brother. I'm sure he is just as nervous as you are," I said, grasping Blake's hand. "It is going to be okay."

There were still tears in his eyes, but when Blake finally smiled, it warmed my heart. A few minutes later, the train came to a stop and the conductor's voice came over the intercom. "All passengers for stop 112, please grab your luggage and head to the front gate." I grabbed my backpack and headed towards the exit with Blake behind me and Ellie leading the way. We got off the train and started to walk up the stairs out of the train station.

"You ready?" I asked.

"Ready as I'll ever be," said Blake with a sigh. None of us really said anything to each other during the three block walk to the Sunshine Set Orphanage. When we got there, Blake practically ran up the steps and knocked on the door.

"Come in," said a sweet voice from the other side of the door. Blake opened the door to see the inside of the building looking fantastic! It looked like a very expensive, high class hotel. There was a brown haired, blue eyed lady sitting at a desk where we had to check in.

"How may I help you?" asked the lady at the desk.

"Uhm, I am looking for Dalton. Dalton Cooper," Blake said in a nervous, but anxious tone.

"And you know him how?" the lady sneered.

"He's my brother," Blake said, almost questioning himself.

"Oh my goodness. I am so very sorry sir. He will be ecstatic to see you! He has been waiting and so has your father!" said the lady, smiling from ear to ear.

"Oh wait. Excuse me! Sorry, but you must have the wrong person. Our father passed away years ago Ma'am," Blake whimpered

"What do you mean? He is upstairs now! I believe he is in the shower! He has lived here with Dalton for over five years now! Jay Cooper, am I correct? I just got hired as their maid only a few months ago and am still learning too honey. I'll go get them now," the lady said, skipping a step here and there as she was running up them so fast.

"What in the hell is happening?" Blake sneered. I couldn't tell if he was going to cry or if he was going to blow up.

"I do not know. I am very confused. She is saying your father has lived here for five years? I thought he was—"

"Uhm, he is. There has got to be a mistake. Maybe she's just a natural blonde and ditsy," Blake said laughing.

"Well there is definitely a problem here," said Ellie.

Just as the three of us had sat down on a bench in front of the desk we heard a voice and turned. "No freakin' way!" It was a voice of a boy.

We heard him when he was halfway down the staircase, just standing there, staring at Blake. I looked at Blake to see him staring back, as if he was dazed. He didn't blink. He didn't move. When I went to shake him he was already starting to stand up. Then they both ran towards each other with their arms wide open, meeting in the center of the room. Me and Ellie stood up slowly, walking towards them still standing there, hugging. As we got right next to them, I saw Blake had his face cuddled into the shoulder of the boy he was hugging. It was him. It was Dalton.

They then pulled away from each other. I saw they both had been sobbing. It was actually kind of cute.

"I missed you so damn much! How are you little bro?" asked Blake as he shoved Dalton's shoulder.

"I'm great, Blake. I thought I'd never see you again. I still can't believe it!" The boy then looked at me and Ellie. "Who are these girls you brought with?" Dalton asked.

"This is my girlfriend, Eva, and her younger sister, Ellie!" Blake shrieked, jumping towards us as he was still wiping away his tears.

I just looked at Blake with a grin. He had never called me his girlfriend to anyone before, at least not when I was around. It felt nice to have some confirmation even though I really didn't need it with everything we have been through. We had to be more than friends now.

"Nice to meet you guys. I am Dalton. I'm sure you've heard all about me," he said with a smile. He looked so much like Blake there was no doubt in my mind they were related.

"Eva," I said holding my hand out.

"Ellie," said my sister, holding out her hand. "I am not sure about your maid or whatever, but she is definitely on something. Not to get in your business, but we have heard enough about Blake to know your father is no longer with us. So why would she bring him up like that to Blake?"

I shoved Ellie with my elbow, giving her a look that asked why would she say that. Maybe she is still riled up about dad and doesn't care anymore. Dalton looked at me, then Ellie, then to Blake. "There is a lot of explaining to do," Dalton said as his face got red.

"I mean obviously it's not true," Blake said as he got closer to Dalton. "We both saw the accident. We both saw what happened to him. What is there to talk about? Tell her the truth Dalton!" Blake yelled.

"Well, well, well, never did I ever think I'd see both of my sons together again!" said a voice from the staircase.

As I looked in that direction, I saw a man standing there with both his arms in the air. "What in the hell?" Blake said as his jaw dropped. Blake just stood there dazed. Dalton stood there crossing his arms, looking back and forth from Blake to the man on the steps.

"D-Dad?" Blake said as his eyes filled with tears.

"W-What happened to you? H-How are you alive?" Blake asked, standing there still dazed and confused. "I mean obviously I'm happy you are, but the accident. You died, Dad. How are you here? Why did you disappear and why didn't either of you jackasses try to find me? I was sleeping in a damn cardboard box while you sat here shoving your faces with food and playing video games?" Blake's voice got louder and louder as he spoke. He started to aggressively point and walk towards Dalton and apparently his dad.

I grabbed Blake's arm and he gave me a light shove away. "What happened and where the hell were you, or for that matter BOTH of you these last few years?" Blake yelled furiously.

"Blake, let me explain. A few days before the accident, I got caught and I didn't want to admit it!" Blake's dad yelled.

"Admit what? Admit what dad?" Blake yelled questioningly.

"I got caught. I had a serious addiction and it led me to start seeing other women. Your mother was so angry with me and I was so angry with myself. You were too young to understand if I was dead or just seriously hurt. I was in a medically induced coma for about six months.

Feeling overwhelmed by the whole situation, your mother gave you both up to foster care and I didn't even have a say. By the time I came out of the coma, I had lost my two sons to foster care and my wife to drugs. I went into hiding for a few years, then started looking for you boys. I found Dalton because he's registered in the system of this center, but you were already eighteen and out of the system, so neither of us knew where to look for you. When Sunnyside went out of business, I saved up to buy the building so we could wait for you here, son. I'm sorry. It's all my fault," said Blake's dad, as tears started to roll down his cheeks. Rather than looking at Blake, I noticed that his dad was staring at the floor the entire time he spoke.

Blake stood there with tears streaming down his cheeks and his hands out in front of him in confusion. He looked at me, then back at his dad, then back at me, then over at his brother.

"Dalton, is what he said true?" Blake questioned.

"I believe him. It all adds up and makes sense, Blake. It's Dad and it's you. We have all found each other. Blake we can be a family again," Dalton said ecstatic, but still kind of upset.

"Dad," Blake whimpered as he walked towards his father with tears in his eyes and his arms out for a hug.

"I missed you bud," Blake's dad said as he hugged Blake, then Dalton joined, followed by me and Ellie.

* * *

Two weeks have passed since we found Dalton. He and Ellie are starting to hit it off now? I'm not sure how I feel about that, but the only thing that matters is that we're all happy.

Me and Ellie are heading back to New York in a few days to visit mom. She has moved in with my aunt. We're going to be there for awhile, and let these boys really get some family alone time.

This has by far been the craziest adventure I have ever been on. Granted, I was stuck in my room for seventeen years, but I still had some crazy adventures to the fridge and real room sometimes. At least I thought.

This is just the beginning of my and Blake's adventure, and I know there will be a lot more to do together. But until then I think I'll be fine hanging out between New York and Connecticut.

So long, see you on the next adventure.

Sigma's Bookshelf (www.SigmasBookshelf.com) is an independent book publishing company that exclusively publishes the work of teenage authors, who are between the ages of 13 and 19. The company was founded in 2016 by Minnesota teenager Justin M. Anderson, whose first book, *Saving Stripes: A Kitty's Story*, was published when he was 14, and has since sold hundreds of copies.

"I know there are a lot of other teenagers out there who are good writers and deserve to have their work published, but don't have access to the kinds of resources I do. I wanted to help them," he said.

Sigma's Bookshelf is a sponsored project of Springboard for the Arts, a nonprofit arts service organization. Contributions on behalf of Sigma's Bookshelf may be made payable to Springboard for the Arts and are tax deductible to the extent permitted by law. Donations can be made online at www.SigmasBookshelf.com/donate.